*For Jess, Louise and Ella -
the most stylish girls in town*

Jamela's Dress copyright © Frances Lincoln Limited 1999
Text and illustrations copyright © Niki Daly 1999
By arrangement with The Inkman, Cape Town, South Africa

Hand–lettering by Andrew van der Merwe

First published in Great Britain in 1999 by
Frances Lincoln Limited, 4 Torriano Mews
Torriano Avenue, London NW5 2RZ

British Library Cataloguing in Publication Data
available on request

ISBN 0-7112-1347-X

Set in Bembo

Printed in Hong Kong
9 8 7 6 5 4 3 2 1

Jamela's Dress

Story & Pictures by
Niki Daly

FRANCES LINCOLN

Mama was very pleased with the new material she'd found at Mnandi's. She had worked hard to earn the money for it.

"It's beautiful, Mama," said Jamela, stroking the crisp new material.

"Yes, it's beautiful. It costs a lot of money – but I need something special to wear for Thelma's wedding," said Mama.

Jamela helped Mama wash the stiffness out of the new material.
Together they hung it out to dry.

"I'll look after it, Mama," said Jamela.

"Thank you," said Mama. "Just make sure Taxi doesn't jump up
and dirty my material."

"Okay," said Jamela.

A warm breeze blew. Jamela rubbed her cheek against the soft
material and followed the beautiful patterns with her finger.
When Taxi barked, Mama called,
    "Jamela, are you looking after my material?"
    "Yes, Mama. It's getting nice and dry," said Jamela.

Dreamily, Jamela swayed between the folds of material as they flapped and wrapped around her into a dress.

When Mama heard nothing going on, she called,
"Are you looking after my material, Jamela?"
There was no answer.

Down the road went Jamela, proud as a peacock,
to show Thelma her beautiful dress for the wedding.

She passed Miss Style and the Snak-Pak Spaza.

"Hi, beautiful!" called old Greasy Hands, who was fixing up
Thelma's wedding car.

Children sang,

Kwela Jamela African Queen!

Taxi barked, and Mrs Zibi's chicken went wild.

Then a boy on a bicycle, who wasn't looking where he was going, went skidding all over Mama's dress material.

What a show!

In his photo studio, Archie heard the commotion.
He ran out clutching his special camera and shouted,
"Hold it, Jamela!"

So Jamela posed. The children pushed in.
Taxi pushed in. Mrs Zibi and her chicken pushed in.
And the boy on the bicycle just s–q–u–e–e–z–e–d in.
They all smiled.

But when Thelma saw Jamela, she scolded,
"Haai, Jamela! Your mama's going to be *verrry* upset
when she sees what you've done with her material."

And Mama was. Mama was so upset that she couldn't even look
at Jamela. She just looked at the dirty, torn material and said sadly,
"What *am* I going to wear for Thelma's wedding?"

Everyone felt sorry for Mama and cross with Jamela. Even Jamela
was cross with Jamela. She hadn't meant to ruin Mama's material.
It had just happened.

A few days later, Archie saw Jamela coming down the road without her usual smile. He called, "Hey Jamela, why so sad? Come see the good news." Pointing to a front-page photograph in the newspaper, Archie read proudly,

"KWELA JAMELA
AFRICAN QUEEN –
*a prize-winning photograph
taken by Archie Khumalo.*"

But instead of looking happy, Jamela started to cry - and she told Archie all about Mama's messed-up material.

"That's a sad, sad story, Jamela," said Archie, "but it has a happy ending." He put his hand into his bag. Jamela wiped her eyes.

"See," said Archie, taking out a bundle of money, "I won a thousand-rand prize for that photograph." Jamela had never seen so much money.

"You can buy lots of things at the shops with that money,
Archie," said Jamela.

"Right!" Archie laughed. "That's the happy ending."

In the afternoon, Archie arrived carrying a gift for
Jamela's mama.

"What is this, Archie?" Mama asked in surprise.

"Open it, Mama, open it!" cried Jamela.

Mama unwrapped the parcel. Inside was a beautiful piece
of material from Mnandi's – just like the first piece.

Jamela jumped up and down.

"*Enkosi kakhulu.* Thank you, Archie!" said Mama.

"No, you must thank Kwela Jamela African Queen,"
said Archie, holding up his prize-winning photograph.

When Mama saw it, she gave Jamela a big hug.

After Archie had gone, Jamela helped Mama
wash the material and hang it out to dry.
"It's the most beautiful material in
the world," said Jamela.
Mama just smiled.
They sang songs as they
watched the feathery patterns
dance in the warm breeze.

Then Mama and Jamela played
a hand-clapping game
for a while.

"Let's do teapots, Mama!" cried Jamela.
So Jamela taught Mama to do
a little song
about a teapot
with a spout.
They dipped
and tipped
and the tea
poured out.

When they stopped, the material felt warm and dry.
So Mama showed Jamela how to fold it just as she
had learnt to do when she was a little girl.

That evening, Mama cut and sewed until she had her special dress to wear to Thelma's wedding. When she had finished, there was a piece of material left over. Mama measured it with her eye, this way and that way. Then she looked at sleeping Jamela, and smiled.

The hands of the clock passed midnight, and Mama was still hard at work. Every now and then she sang softly to herself, "Kwela Jamela African Queen."

Next day at the wedding, Thelma looked radiant,

Mama looked lovely,

and when Archie said, "Smile, everyone!"
guess who had the biggest smile?

Kwela Jamela African Queen!

– that's who!